Curly-Mons

in Rocky Rolly Party

Scholastic Children's Books
Scholastic Publications Ltd
7-9 Pratt Street, London NW1 0AE, UK

Scholastic Inc
730 Broadway, New York, NY 10003, USA

Scholastic Canada Ltd
123 Newkirk Road, Richmond Hill
Ontario, Canada L4C 3G5

Ashton Scholastic Pty Ltd
PO Box 579, Gosford, New South Wales
Australia

Ashton Scholastic Ltd
Private Bag 1, Penrose, Auckland
New Zealand

First published by Scholastic Publications Ltd, 1993
Copyright © Frank Rodgers, 1993

ISBN: 0 590 55313 5

Typeset by Rapid Reprographics, London

Printed and bound in Belgium by Proost Book Production.

10 9 8 7 6 5 4 3 2 1

Curly-top Monster

in

Rocky Rolly Party

Frank Rodgers

Monsters never need an excuse to have a party...

so when Curly-top Monster suggested having a
fancy-dress party all the Monsters thought it was
a wonderful idea.

Everyone helped.

Ring-tailed Monster made delicious mud-covered doughnuts...

Hairy Monster
tried out
the party
games...

and Curly-top Monster was in charge of the dancing.

"Hmmm," thought Curly-top Monster, "what kind of dancing will we have?"

"Ballet dancing?
No...not enough
silly fun!

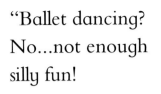

Ballroomy dancing?
No...not enough
jumpy fun!"

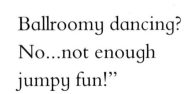

Curly-top Monster thought hard. "What kind of dancing has lots of silly *and* jumpy fun?"

Suddenly he snapped his fingers. "I know! Rock and Rolly! We'll have Rock and Rolly dancing at the party!"

Curly-top Monster was so pleased with his idea
that he wound up the Monsters' old record-
player and put on a Rock and Rolly record so
he could practise.

"Rock 'n Roll me, Baby!" screamed the record.

"Rocky Rolly, maybe!" yelled Curly-top
Monster.

Unfortunately, the mud-mound was rather small and Curly-top Monster was rather large.

WHOOOOPS!
He slipped
on a rug...

BOINK!
he bumped
into the
record-
player...

CRASH! He fell on top of it.

"I think I've broken it," said Curly-top Monster
as the other Monsters looked in anxiously.

Hairy Monster shook his head. "Wrecked
player," he said. "Last one in the swamp. It
means no dancing at the party."

15

Suddenly Curly-top Monster had an idea. "We'll make our own music!" he exclaimed.

"Like the idea!" chorused the Monsters and rushed off to get their instruments.

Two minutes later they were back.

Furry Monster had brought his drums but was wearing ear-plugs as he didn't like loud noises. Hairy Monster had a guitar with two strings and Ring-tailed Monster had an old trumpet.

The other Monsters had brought anything they could find.

Curly-top Monster raised his hands. "When I count to four," he said, "begin. One, two...er..."

"Three?" suggested Hairy Monster.

"Er...yes, three, thank you," said Curly-top
Monster. "Three and...four!"
All the Monsters began playing at top volume.

"Stop!" yelled Curly-top Monster.

Everyone stopped.

"Was it any good?" they asked hopefully.

"Good?" shouted Curly-top Monster. "It was sillyjumpy and rocky rolly and FABURRIFIC!"

The Monsters beamed. Yes, it had been rather good, they thought.

But then Curly-top Monster frowned, "Trouble is," he said, "if we all play music...
who will dance?"

Furry Monster shook his head. "Can't play drums *and* dance," he said. "Imposterous!"

Some Monsters tried to play and dance at the same time but when Lesser-spotted Monster nearly swallowed her whistle they decided it wasn't a good idea and went home.

Curly-top Monster was left alone so he went for a walk in the swamp to think.

As he wandered through the swamp he met a
rooster and two hens.

"Hello," said Curly-top Monster politely.

"Rock-a-doodle-doo!" replied the rooster.

"Er...shouldn't that be *Cock*-a-doodle-doo?"
asked Curly-top Monster.

"Raaawk!" nodded
the rooster.
"Cluck! Cluck!"
agreed the
hens.

"Could you repeat that?" asked Curly-top
Monster. "Raaawk!" said the rooster obligingly.
"Cluck! Cluck!" added the hens.

It sounded so musical that Curly-top Monster
had *another* idea.

That evening, all the Monsters were having a wonderful fancy-dress rocky rolly party.

Just as they thought they would have to finish without having a dance Curly-top Monster sprang his surprise.

"Monsters all!" he announced. "I present the most rocky and rolly band in the swamp...Me, Rocky Rooster and the Henettes!

Are you ready? Are you steady? Then one, two... er...three, FOUR!"

RAAWK!

CLUCK! CLUCK!

COCK-A-DOODLE!

ROLL!

CLUCK! CLUCK!

ROCK
-A-
DOODLE!

The Monsters snapped their fingers, clapped their hands, bumped their tails and tapped their toes. They liked it.

By the time the band had started the second
verse, (which was exactly the same as the first)
the Monsters were dancing.

"Hooray for Rocky Rooster and the Henettes and hooray for Curly-top Monster!" they cheered. "Rock-a-doodle, cock-a-doodle, ROCK-A-DOODLE DOOO!"